FISHERMEN
THROUGH & THROUGH

Colleen Sydor • Illustrated by Brooke Kerrigan

Red Deer Press

There once lived three fishermen: Peter, Santiago, and Ahab. They were tough. They were as salty as the bottom of a pretzel bag. They were as weathered as a twisted stick of driftwood. Yes, these three were fishermen through and through.

Which is not to say that they didn't sometimes dream of things other than fish, knotted nets, and saltwater.

Peter had heard of entire countries covered in vast seas of sand that spread farther than a body can imagine. He dreamed of one day sailing a golden desert on the back of a camel.

Santiago's attentions soared all the way to his feathered pals in the sky. He watched them gliding in a vast sea of clouds stretching farther than a body can dream. He longed to sail the sky in a balloon and gaze at his beloved sea with the eyes of a gull.

And Ahab? Even though Ahab's favorite color was the blue-green-gray of the sea, he had once seen a photograph of endless fields of rainbow tulips in Holland. What he wouldn't have given for his eyes to sail a vast sea of wind-tossed flowers as far as a body could know!

And even though they were weathered and salty and tough as the barnacles on the bottom of their boat, on dreamy days when the sea was gentle, they were known to talk of such things as sand dunes and clouds and tulips.

It was on one of these dreamy days that, as they drew in their nets, they saw something as unlikely as a rolling ocean of tulips beneath their rudder. They wondered at first if the sun was playing tricks. But as sure as there are sunfish in the ocean, they saw, nestled among the dark blue crabs and glinting scales of silver fish, a lobster as white as the clouds in Santiago's daydreams.

Blow me down!

Peter carefully untangled the lily lobster from the nets while Santiago emptied their large bait bucket and Ahab filled it with seawater.

The three fishermen stared in silent wonder, for they weren't so weathered and salty and tough that they didn't recognize beauty when they found it doing the front crawl in their bucket.

The white lobster stared back with equal wonder, for never in its life had it seen anything quite like these three strange creatures with neither shells nor scales.

Man and crustacean sailed this way, admiring one another until the sun got snoozey and drifted down, down on an orange cloud, toward the lip of the sea. As Santiago made ready to return the white lobster to the water, Peter raised his hand. "Wait! Perhaps we are being a little selfish?"

Ahab and Santiago understood. Why should theirs be the only eyes to have marveled at this amazing miracle?

Indeed.

Once they had docked their boat and taken care of the day's catch, the three fishermen trudged heavily up the hill taking turns between them carrying the bucket.

They stopped when they reached a restaurant called the Fisherman's Net and they stayed long enough to see their new amigo set up grandly in its own glass tank of seawater.

They watched the expressions of awe and delight on the faces of customers who dropped into the Fisherman's Net for a cup of coffee and left with a memory they wouldn't soon forget.

Surely they had done the right thing.

Eventually the customers of the Fisherman's Net began to wonder if they weren't being a tad selfish with their white secret. Surely others would delight in seeing what, so far, only their eyes had beheld.

When word of the albino lobster began to travel, so did photographers, marine biologists, newsmen — and even a man from *Ripley's Believe it or Not* — to gawk at this rare creature. The fishermen were kept busy for three days with radio interviews and television appearances and long cups of coffee with news reporters and locals who were enjoying the fishermen's fame.

Santiago, Peter and Ahab were even offered money for the lobster (as if it was theirs to sell!).

When Peter said, "No," the offer was doubled and when Santiago said, "No," it was tripled.

Then the buyer offered an amount that silenced the "No" about to slip from Ahab's lips.

Instead, his mouth dropped open in amazement, for that sum of money would more than allow Peter to sail a sea of sand, Ahab a sea of clouds, and Santiago a sea of flowers as far as a body could see.

Blow me down.

What were they to do?

They spent that night in their small homes dreaming more clearly
than ever of golden sand, rainbow tulips, and pink sunset clouds.
They might as well have been there. (And maybe they were?)
    But their sleep was fitful and all three found
themselves waking often to the sounds of the night.

Santiago yawned and listened to his complaining feet. Not in a very long time had they been planted on firm ground for such a long stretch. They sorely craved the rolling swell that only a boat's bottom at sea could provide.

Ahab, meanwhile, was listening to owls and nighthawks outside his window. Three days away from his beloved seagulls had left him lonely.

In his small cottage, Peter listened to the distant
thrum of waves kissing the shore before rushing
back out to sea. Finally he put his coat on over his
pajamas, and, like the waves, rushed seaward.

Blow me down if he didn't see two familiar old salts on the shore with bare feet and pajama bottoms wet with surf. All three stood silently trying to imagine life without the sea. When they finally pulled their glances away from the waves and looked at one another, their sad eyes began to twinkle and wrinkle at the corners to make room for knowing grins.

Joe, the owner of the Fisherman's Net restaurant never did find out who his open-window, midnight visitors had been. And he puzzled forever about why they had chosen to take the white lobster instead of the stacks of money that the famous crustacean had brought to his till.

Joe was glad — and not because he still had his money! As a child he had kept a beautiful butterfly in a fish bowl with a plastic bag lid, until the Monarch folded its wings and lay lifeless on the bottom. The sight of that empty aquarium seemed as beautiful to Joe as a lidless fish bowl.

He went back to bed and dreamt of a butterfly landing gently on his nose before taking to the skies.

And the three fishermen?

As you know, they were tough and as salty as three wrinkled pickles in a very old jar. No tears or sad farewells from these tough-as-barnacles sailors! They simply said, "Welcome home," and smiled as they heard the splash. Then they watched, flashlights in hand, as the white lobster turned first to yellow, then green, then brown as it slowly sank out of sight.

For they weren't wrinkled pickles in a jar. They were fishermen through and through; yes, born fishermen through and through.

Published in Canada by Red Deer Press, 195 Allstate Parkway, Markham, Ontario L3R 4T8

Published in the United States by Red Deer Press, 311 Washington Street, Brighton, Massachusetts 02135

All inquiries should be addressed to Red Deer Press, 195 Allstate Parkway, Markham, Ontario L3R 4T8   www.reddeerpress.com

10 9 8 7 6 5 4 3 2 1

Red Deer Press acknowledges with thanks the Canada Council for the Arts, and the Ontario Arts Council for their support of our publishing program. We acknowledge the financial support of the Government of Canada through the Canada Book Fund (CBF) for our publishing activities.

ONTARIO ARTS COUNCIL
CONSEIL DES ARTS DE L'ONTARIO
an Ontario government agency
un organisme du gouvernement de l'Ontario

Canada Council   Conseil des arts
for the Arts   du Canada

Library and Archives Canada Cataloguing in Publication
Sydor, Colleen, author
    Fishermen through and through / Colleen Sydor ; illustrations by Brooke Kerrigan.
Issued in print and electronic formats.
ISBN 978-0-88995-517-2 (bound).--ISBN 978-1-55244-350-7 (pdf)
    I. Kerrigan, Brooke, illustrator II. Title.
PS8587.Y36F57 2014   jC813'.54   C2014-904730-4
                                               C2014-904731-2

Publisher Cataloging-in-Publication Data (U.S.)
Sydor, Colleen.
    Fisherman through and through / Colleen Sydor ; illustrations by Brooke Kerrigan.
[32] pages : color illustrations ;   cm.
Summary: Three fishermen with dreams of exotic places make an extra special catch one day: an albino lobster which they put on display for the people in their village. When offered big money that would allow them to fulfill their dreams, they decide it's impossible to imagine their lives without the sea and the sound of the gulls overhead, and return the lobster to its ocean.
ISBN-13: 978-0-88995-517-2
Also published in electronic formats.
1. Fishers – Juvenile fiction. I. Kerrigan, Brooke. II. Title.

[E] dc23   PZ7. 2014

Edited for the Press by Peter Carver
Text design, cover design, and cover illustration by Brooke Kerrigan
Printed in China by Sheck Wah Tong Printing Press Ltd.

Thanks to Bill Coopersmith (junior and senior), for one day taking an albino lobster from the ocean, naming him Lincoln, and then kindly putting him back, thereby providing me with the inspiration to write this story. Thank you, Bill Coopersmith! Long may Lincoln live!

— Colleen Sydor

For Lincoln and his fishermen friends — CS
For Olive, with love — BK